# NICK DEAR

# Frankenstein

*based on the novel by*
MARY SHELLEY

*faber and faber*

First published in 2011
by Faber and Faber Ltd
74–77 Great Russell Street
London WC1B 3DA

Typeset by Country Setting, Kingsdown, Kent CT14 8ES
Printed in England by CPI Bookmarque, Croydon, Surrey

Nick Dear is hereby identified as author
of this work in accordance with Section 77 of the
Copyright, Designs and Patents Act 1988

A CIP record for this book
is available from the British Library

ISBN 978-0-571-27721-6

2 4 6 8 10 9 7 5 3 1

For Joanna Marston

7

Frankenstein was first presented on the Olivier stage
of the National Theatre, London, on 5 February 2011.
The cast, in order of speaking, was as follows:

**Victor Frankenstein/The Creature**
  Benedict Cumberbatch, Jonny Lee Miller
**Gretel/Clarice** Ella Smith
**Gustav/Constable** John Killoran
**Klaus** Steven Elliott
**De Lacey** Karl Johnson
**Felix** Daniel Millar
**Agatha** Lizzie Winkler
**Female Creature** Andreea Padurariu
**Elizabeth Lavenza** Naomie Harris
**William Frankenstein** Haydon Downing/
  William Nye
**Monsieur Frankenstein** George Harris
**Servant 1** Daniel Ings
**Servant 2** Martin Chamberlain
**Ewan** John Stahl
**Rab** Mark Armstrong
**Ensemble** Josie Daxter

*Director* Danny Boyle
*Designer* Mark Tildesley
*Costume Designer* Suttirat Larlarb
*Lighting Designer* Bruno Poet
*Music and Soundscore* Underworld
*Sound Designer* Mike Walker
*Director of Movement* Toby Sedgwick
*Fight Director* Kate Waters

# Characters

**The Creature**

**Victor Frankenstein**
a scientist

**Gretel**
a prostitute

**Gustav**
a beggar

**Klaus**
a beggar

**De Lacey**
a blind man

**Felix**
his son

**Agatha**
his daughter-in-law

**The Female Creature**

**Elizabeth Lavenza**
Victor's fiancée

**Clarice**
her maid

**William Frankenstein**
Victor's brother

**Monsieur Frankenstein**
Victor's father

**Ewan**
an Orkney islander

**Rab**
his nephew

**A Constable**

**Townspeople**
of Ingolstadt

**Servants**
of the Frankenstein household

# FRANKENSTEIN

## SCENE ONE

*Europe, around 1818.*

*Darkness. There's the sound of a heartbeat.*
BOM-BOOM.
*Then another heartbeat, then another:* BOM-BOOM.
BOM-BOOM.
*Sudden flash of brilliant white light. There is a vertical frame on which something like a human form is suspended. It moves. Rubber tubes, like drips, are inserted into it at various points.*
*Back to darkness.*

BOM-BOOM. BOM-BOOM. BOM-BOOM.
*Another blast of light. Struggling to free himself is the Creature, who is naked and leaking blood as he rips the tubes out of his veins.*
BOM-BOOM. BOM-BOOM.
*Then darkness.*

*Light: the Creature has got down from the frame. He squats on the floor. He seems confused. He has no speech and his movements are erratic. Spurts of blood come from the sutures in his skin.*
*It goes dark again. Now we realise what's happening: it gets light when he opens his eyes.*
*The Creature seems to realise this too. He puts a hand clumsily to his eye. He holds it open. It stays light. He lets his hand fall and his eye closes again. It gets dark. With both hands he forces his eyes open and holds them open.*
*It gets light and it stays light.*

## SCENE TWO

*The Creature crawls across the floor. He is in a dingy garret. He hauls himself shakily to his feet. He struggles to keep his balance and take a few steps.*

*He falls. He lies still. Then he tries again.*

*He pads back and forth uncertainly, taking harsh little breaths. He is made in the image of a man, as if by an amateur god. All the parts are there, but the neurological pathways are unorthodox, the muscular movements odd, the body and the brain uncoordinated.*

*He licks at the blood on his skin.*

## SCENE THREE

*The Creature plays with a kettle, sitting on the floor. He chews it and bangs it.*

*The Creature spins like a top, on his tailbone, pushing himself round and round and round. And round and round some more.*

*He stands, and is dizzy. He falls over. He laughs.*

*A man is approaching slowly and cautiously: Victor Frankenstein, late twenties. He wears a long cloak. He watches the Creature intently.*

*Victor goes close to the Creature, who doesn't see him at first. Victor is curious, but then repulsed by the filthy, slimy being sprawled in front of him.*

*The Creature turns and sees Victor. He reaches out to him, babbling incoherently. He gives a ghastly smile. Victor is appalled. He backs off.*

*The Creature pursues Victor, moving swiftly across the floor.*

**Victor** No . . . keep away . . . no . . .

*The Creature gets to his feet – and now Victor is worried.*

**Creature** Hawuurgh!

**Victor** Do as I say!

*The Creature lunges at Victor, as if to embrace him, or maybe to strangle him – who knows? Victor panics. He has nothing with which to defend himself. He pulls the cloak from his shoulders and throws it over the Creature, and runs from the building.*

*Blinded, the Creature roars, spinning round and round, confused. He pulls the cloak from his head. But Victor is gone.*

### SCENE FOUR

*Night. The Creature makes his way through the streets of Ingolstadt – an early-industrial landscape, smoggy and strange.*

*He's wrapped in the cloak, the cowl covering his head. Underneath he is naked.*

*There are strange noises – sounds of forges, factories, coaches, animals. Electricity is in the air; we see prototypes of new machines. The Creature is lost and confused. There are passers-by, but they ignore him.*

*He passes a tavern. A group of townsmen are singing, drinking mugs of beer. This scares the Creature and he runs away.*

*Then there is a sound which arrests him: a woman is screaming.*

**Gretel** Help! Help!

*The Creature stops and listens. The passers-by slip away. He is alone on the street.*

**Creature** Hnungh?

*Now we see Gretel, a prostitute, being beaten up by her client in a dark alley.*

**Gretel** Please, help me! Someone!

*The Creature doesn't know how to respond. He turns this way and that. Gretel is being thrown about by her hair. The Creature walks slowly towards them and watches with curiosity. Gretel sees him.*

Oh, thank you, mister, thank you!

*The client looks round and sees the Creature behind him. The Creature raises both hands in the air and spins round and round. It's scary – unintentionally so. The client dumps Gretel on the ground and runs. She picks herself up and dusts down her skirts. She doesn't get a good look at the Creature yet.*

One good turn deserves another. Want to come with me? I've got wine. We can drink.

*She swigs from a flagon of wine, and beckons him.*

Come closer. What's your name? I'm Gretel.

*The Creature goes to her and immediately drops to his knees and puts his nose to her vagina and sniffs, hard.*

Here, what are you playing at? Give us a kiss, at least! Christ!

*Gretel pulls him to his feet and pushes back the cowl from his head. She goes to kiss him – but then she sees his face. She gasps, and takes a step backwards.*
*The Creature stands with his arms at his sides, smiling. Gretel backs away slowly, trying to stay as calm as she can.*

I'm not going to scream. I'm just going to walk away.

All right, mister? Just walking away. All right?

*Finally Gretel turns and runs. The Creature doesn't
notice. He's busy examining the wine she left behind.
He takes a swig. He spits it out: it's disgusting.*


## SCENE FIVE

*The Creature is on the outskirts of the town. Dogs bark.
He turns to look back. In the distance we can see the
lights and towers of Ingolstadt.*

*Several townsmen run towards him. They keep their
distance. The Creature stares at them uncertainly.*

**Man** There it is!

*They throw stones at him, and he turns and runs.*


## SCENE SIX

*Dawn. Countryside. The Creature is asleep on the ground,
wrapped in the cloak.*

*He wakes, stiffly. He moans and sits up.*

*He stands and looks around. The cloak falls and he is
naked. Sunlight plays through the leaves. The birds sing.
He clutches at beams of light. He laughs.*

**Creature** Huh, huh!

*He's Adam in the Garden of Eden – an innocent.
He listens to the birdsong. He tries to flap his wings.
    He imitates birdsong.*

*Rain falls. The gentle touch of moisture pleases
him. He washes himself in the rain. He dries himself
with his cloak.*

## SCENE SEVEN

*The Creature wanders through the woods. He has a
collection of things to eat, which he tries one by one.
Sticks are not very nice. Weeds are chewy. Best of all are
berries. Juice runs down his chin.*

## SCENE EIGHT

*The Creature sits under a tree. He fidgets. He's bored.*
*In the pocket of his cloak he finds a battered notebook:
Frankenstein's journal. He looks at the writing from
several different viewpoints but it remains meaningless.
He stuffs it back into his pocket.*

*He stands and addresses us: a speech of confusion and
sometimes distress, but without actual words. A soliloquy
of grunts and wails.*

**Creature** Wurrgh – ah – ah! Wurgh, wurgh. Chick chick.
Awah? Yaya yaya! Yuh!

*Seeming to have made his point, he leaves.*

## SCENE NINE

*Night. A beggar, Gustav, comes through the woods.*

**Gustav** (*calls*) Klaus? Where are you?

*Klaus, another beggar, is tending a fire.*

**Klaus** Over here! Come and get warm.

**Gustav** I will. – What's in the pot?

**Klaus** Nice bit of rabbit. Where'd you get to?

**Gustav** Ingolstadt.

**Klaus** Any luck?

**Gustav** No. They're jittery as hell. The women and children are locked indoors. The men go armed with cudgels. What's going on?

**Klaus** (*shrugs*) Scared of their own shadows, they are, in Ingolstadt.

*They laugh and sit by the fire. Klaus stirs the stew in the billy-can.*

**Gustav** Tomorrow we'll move on. Try and beg some bread.

**Klaus** This is all right, though, nice bit of rabbit.

**Gustav** A man needs bread.

**Klaus** I met a woman in Augsburg once, her husband was a baker. I hung around Augsburg for a very long time.

**Gustav** Nice place, Augsburg.

**Klaus** Very nice place. Welcoming.

*The Creature approaches, drawn to the firelight.*

**Creature** Gnnah.

*The beggars leap to their feet. The Creature advances towards them. They pull back, scared.*

**Gustav** What's that? What is it?

**Klaus** I don't know!

**Gustav** (*waving his arms*) Piss off! Bugger off!

**Klaus** Watch out!

**Creature** Gnnah! Gnnah!

*The Creature points to the pan of food hanging over the fire.*

**Klaus** Run! Quick!

**Gustav** But the food –

**Klaus** Leave it, Gustav! Run!

**Gustav** A monster! Piss off! Bugger off!

**Klaus** Look at the state of him!

**Gustav** Run!

*The beggars run away. The Creature tries to pick up the pan, but it's hot and burns his hand. He yelps with pain. But he wants the food. He experiments with the wooden spoon. He finds that with it he can bring food to his mouth. He eats. Now he examines the fire. It's nice. But when he puts his hand in it, it's not nice.*

*He sees that the beggars have left their knapsacks behind. He pulls out the contents – tattered clothes, a ball of string, a pipe, a Bible. None of these mean much to him.*

*He lies down by the fire and goes to sleep.*

### SCENE TEN

*Morning. The Creature wakes to the sound of the two beggars yelling. They run at him, brandishing sticks.*

**Klaus** There he is! Get him!

*They attack the Creature and beat him savagely.*

**Creature** Waaagh!

**Gustav** I'll teach you to scare us!

**Klaus** Eat our supper!

**Gustav** Now piss off, you ugly bastard!

**Klaus** And don't come back!

*They drive the Creature away. The beggars collect up their belongings and exit hurriedly.*

### SCENE ELEVEN

*Deep in the woods, the Creature howls with pain. He is angry and confused. He spins round and round, shrieking in anguish.*

### SCENE TWELVE

*De Lacey's cottage. Felix, his son, guides blind De Lacey to his chair, as his daughter-in-law Agatha places food on the table.*

**Agatha** I'm leaving your food on the table. And there's some milk.

**De Lacey** Thank you, my dear. You treat me well.

**Felix** We're going to work, Father. We'll be back at nightfall.

**Agatha** (*to De Lacey*) And you, behave yourself while we're gone.

**De Lacey** (*chuckles*) I'll try. – Have you managed to clear the top field?

**Felix** No. It's slow progress.

**Agatha** Harder than we thought. (*Cheerily.*) But we'll win in the end!

**De Lacey** We have to grow something or we'll starve.

**Agatha** We'll get faster when we know what we're doing. In a year or two, we'll be fine. We'll be farmers!

**De Lacey** (*laughs*) I never thought I'd be a farmer . . .!

**Felix** (*to Agatha*) Are you ready?

**Agatha** For the cold and the mud? Can't wait!

*She laughs, and kisses De Lacey affectionately.*

Bye, old man!

**Felix** Goodbye, Father.

**De Lacey** Goodbye, Felix. You married a lovely girl.

**Felix** I know.

**Agatha** Bye!

*Agatha and Felix exit the hut. De Lacey reaches behind him and takes up a guitar. He puts it across his knee and begins to play.*
*Felix and Agatha come outside. The Creature looks on from a distance. He now wears ragged clothes under his cloak. He watches intently.*

**Felix** How do you manage to stay so cheerful?

**Agatha** What choice is there? This is where we've ended up, this is what we have to do. Come on!

**Felix** Agatha. Do you know how beautiful you are? I swear I will love you for ever.

**Agatha** You'd better!

**Felix** (*kisses her, strokes her hair*) When will you give me a son, beautiful wife?

**Agatha** (*laughs and pulls away*) Come! We've work to do!

*Felix and Agatha exit, hand in hand.*

*The Creature watches them go. Very cautiously he makes his way to the hut. He hovers in the doorway, captivated by the guitar music. De Lacey, hearing something, stops playing.*

**De Lacey** Take the food if you want it. There's nothing else worth taking. Oh, there are books, I suppose. At least they have left me my books.

*De Lacey leans his guitar against the wall. The Creature seems to grasp that he's not in danger.*

You've no reason to harm me. I won't hurt you. I can't see you. I don't fight on any side. Go on, citizen, take the food.

**Creature** Hnnargh?

*De Lacey indicates the table. The Creature stuffs food in his mouth.*

**De Lacey** Can't you talk? Maybe you can't. It's nothing to be ashamed of. Look at me – I'm blind. There was a cannonball and I – I went blind. Now my son looks after me. You look after them when they're little, they look after you when you're old. That's the way it is. But we fell on hard times, when the soldiers came through. When people are not oppressed, they're full of brotherly love; but when times are hard . . . well, then you find out who your friends are, don't you?

*The Creature, having finished the food, picks up the guitar. He tries clumsily to strum it, but just makes a horrible noise. He claws hopelessly at the strings, then cries out in frustration.*

**Creature** Waaarh! Pissoff buggeroff!

**De Lacey** I beg your pardon?

**Creature** Pissoff buggeroff!

*The Creature plonks the guitar down in De Lacey's lap.*

**De Lacey** Oh, you want music? You want some more music?

**Creature** Mm . . . moo . . .

**De Lacey** Music. It's a gift from God. Go on. Say it. Music.

**Creature** Moo . . . sic . . .

**De Lacey** You see, you pluck the strings, like this . . .

*De Lacey plays the guitar. The Creature listens, transported.*

### SCENE THIRTEEN

*Agatha and Felix survey the top field. Felix carries a hoe over his shoulder.*

**Agatha** Look at the stones! The field is full of them!

**Felix** I'm sorry, Agatha. It has to be cleared. I can't plough until it's done.

**Agatha** Oh well – the sooner I start!

*She smiles and kisses Felix. Felix exits. Agatha begins to work. She sings.*
    *She has the feeling that she's being watched. But when she looks round, she can't see anyone.*
    *Agatha remains working in the field as we cut back to:*

*The cottage. The Creature and De Lacey sit together at*
*the table. They have paper and charcoal pencils before*
*them. De Lacey scrawls a letter and the Creature*
*imitates him.*

**De Lacey** Puh.

**Creature** Puh.

**De Lacey** Ah.

**Creature** Ah.

**De Lacey** Ruh.

**Creature** Ruh.

**De Lacey** Ah.

**Creature** Ah.

**De Lacey** Duh.

**Creature** Duh.

**De Lacey** Aye.

**Creature** Aye.

**De Lacey** Sss.

**Creature** Sss.

**De Lacey** Eh.

**Creature** Eh.

*De Lacey puts down his charcoal.*

**De Lacey** Para –

**Creature** Para –

**De Lacey** – dise. Paradise. Write it out.

*The Creature writes.*

**Creature** Paradise. My like. Nice word.

*De Lacey reaches out to touch his face. The Creature flinches.*

**De Lacey** Don't be afraid. This is how I see. Please?

*De Lacey feels the Creature's head. The Creature is at first tense, but then relaxes.*

**Creature** Gurrurrgh, eheh.

**De Lacey** My, you have been in the wars. What happened to you? Where are you from? Where are your mother and father?

*The Creature has lost interest, and concentrates happily on his writing.*

**Creature** Par – a – dise. Hnagh!

*De Lacey sighs. They stay in the cottage as we cut back to:*


### SCENE FIFTEEN

*The fields. Agatha is in high excitement.*

**Agatha** Felix! Felix!

*Felix runs to her.*

**Felix** What is it?

**Agatha** Look, just look!

*Felix surveys the field, and gasps.*

**Felix** But that's –

**Agatha**  It's incredible! It's a miracle!

**Felix**  Or magic.

**Agatha**  Every stone is gone! Every one!

**Felix**  We can till the soil!

**Agatha**  We can sow.

**Felix**  Help me hitch up the plough!

*They exit. We cut back to:*


### SCENE SIXTEEN

*The cottage. Weeks later. De Lacey and the Creature.
The Creature is distracted by the snow swirling outside
the window.*

**Creature**  White! What? White! What?

**De Lacey**  Where?

**Creature**  In the air!

**De Lacey**  That's snow. It's not very interesting – a
natural phenomenon, no more. Now please stop leaping
about, we need to concentrate.

**Creature**  Snow! Snow!

**De Lacey**  Sit! We've work to do.

*The Creature sits at a pile of books, rather grumpily.*

Thank you. Today: original sin.

**Creature**  (*writing, with a scowl*) Original sin.

**De Lacey**  There are two schools of thought. One says
that we are all made imperfect, and require the assistance
of a higher authority – a deity – to overcome the sin of

being born. The other school of thought – to which I subscribe – insists that when we leave the womb we are pure, that a babe in arms is untainted by sin, that evil is the product of social forces, and that God has nothing to do with how a man turns out, be it good or be it bad.

**Creature** Me not do bad things.

**De Lacey** I know you do not do bad things. You have a good heart. I know that.

**Creature** Why my hungry?

**De Lacey** Eh?

**Creature** Why my hungry? Why no food for me?

**De Lacey** I give you half of my food.

**Creature** Still hungry.

**De Lacey** It is the condition of men to be hungry.

**Creature** (*jabbing a finger at his books*) Not kings! Not emperors!

**De Lacey** (*laughs*) You're learning fast.

**Creature** Why my not a king?

**De Lacey** I don't know. Perhaps you are.

**Creature** Yes! A king! Is my name?

**De Lacey** I don't know.

**Creature** King what?

**De Lacey** You have never told me your name.

**Creature** Gnaaagh! Never heard. Not know.

**De Lacey** You are a poor lost thing.

**Creature** Lost thing.

**De Lacey** But I have taught you how to speak! How to read! There is hope. Who knows what you may accomplish?

**Creature** (*shakes his head*) Hate me.

**De Lacey** Who does?

**Creature** Men. Women. Childs. Dogs.

**De Lacey** No, they don't.

**Creature** Throw stones. Beat me. Everywhere! Everywhere!

**De Lacey** Peasants are ignorant people. They do not read like you and I. It's an instinct to protect the home, the family. Perhaps they are – frightened of you?

**Creature** My look bad?

*De Lacey is silent.*

Not like Agatha.

**De Lacey** Agatha?

**Creature** Beautiful wife!

**De Lacey** Well, Agatha is beautiful, certainly – and Felix is kind. Let me introduce you to them.

**Creature** No.

**De Lacey** Why not?

**Creature** Hate me.

**De Lacey** No, they don't! They've never met you! Stay, and greet them, when they come home.

*The Creature jumps up and runs outside.*

**Creature** Snow! Snow! Snow!

*He exits. We cut back to:*

## SCENE SEVENTEEN

*The field. Agatha and Felix enter from different directions.*

**Felix** Agatha – look what I found!

**Agatha** And me – look what I found!

*Felix is dragging a huge bundle of chopped firewood.*

**Felix** It's all chopped – ready for the fire! It was lying at the foot of the field.

*Agatha carries two dead pheasants in one hand, and two dead hares in the other.*

**Agatha** These were left by the stove – the hares already gutted! Not a mark on the birds.

**Felix** Then how were they caught?

**Agatha** It's a mystery! Who is doing this, Felix?

**Felix** Somebody wants to help us.

**Agatha** But who? Who would do that? We are strangers here.

**Felix** (*whispers*) Faerie folk.

**Agatha** Faerie folk?

**Felix** Little people! Elves and sprites! (*Calls.*) Hello! Are you there?

**Agatha** (*calls*) Is anyone watching?

*Now we see that the Creature is indeed watching from a hiding place.*

**Felix** Come out if you are! We'd like to thank you! Come out!

*The Creature is very tempted and almost steps out of cover. But something holds him back.*

They won't come out.

**Agatha** (*laughs*) There's no one there, you fool. It's just us. You see? We stick together through thick and thin, and never stop loving each other – and magical things happen!

*They kiss and exit. The Creature smiles happily to himself.*

## SCENE EIGHTEEN

*Months later. The Creature gives his arm to De Lacey, and they walk in the woods. It's evening – the light is fading. A single bird calls, as a huge moon rises.*

**De Lacey** The evenings grow warmer. Soon it will be spring. There's a cheery thought!

**Creature** Why?

**De Lacey** Well – spring, you know! Ha ha!

**Creature** Spring makes you happy? Why?

**De Lacey** Well, we're still alive!

**Creature** Why, how long are we meant to be alive for?

**De Lacey** Let's turn for home now. It's getting dark.

**Creature** How can you tell? You have no eyes.

**De Lacey** Hear that bird? It's a nightingale. That means it's getting dark.

**Creature** The bird makes the dark? That's impossible.

**De Lacey** No, my friend, no. Don't you remember your Milton? 'The wakeful nightingale . . .'

**Creature** The wakeful nightingale!

*He recites.*

'She all night long her amorous descant sung;
Silence was pleased: now glowed the firmament
With living sapphires: Hesperus, that led
The starry host, rode brightest, till the moon,
Rising in clouded majesty, at length
Apparent queen unveiled her peerless light,
And o'er the dark her silver mantle threw.'

**De Lacey** (*approving*) It is night in the Garden of Eden.
Do you see the moon?

**Creature** There. There it is.

**De Lacey** Describe it to me.

**Creature** Solitary.

**De Lacey** That's a good word. Good.

**Creature** And sad, like me.

**De Lacey** Why is it sad?

**Creature** Because it is solitary.

**De Lacey** Why are you sad?

**Creature** Because with all that I read, all that I learn, I
discover how much I do not know. Ideas batter me like
hailstones. Questions but no answers. Who am I? Where
am I from? Do I have a family?

**De Lacey** You have us. My son will not turn you away,
I promise you. Come along and say hello to him.

**Creature** No!

**De Lacey** But why not? It's a simple request. What is
your –?

*The Creature suddenly shoves De Lacey and leaves his side.*

**Creature** Do not request it again.

*De Lacey staggers, and recovers his balance. But he cannot see where he is. The Creature keeps his distance.*

I have been reading Plutarch. *The Lives of the Emperors.*

**De Lacey** Ah, yes, the founders of ancient Rome – men who showed that the world could be improved!

**Creature** Why do men live in herds in cities? I cannot imagine a city. I cannot imagine Rome! The numbers are too great.

**De Lacey** We band together to help one another, and do good.

**Creature** But then you massacre each other!

**De Lacey** Yes, it's inconsistent.

*The Creature spins round a couple of times.*

**Creature** I do not like inconsistent! Why must it be so?

**De Lacey** I don't know. That's the way it is.

**Creature** But how do I find out the way that it is?

**De Lacey** I don't know. As you get older, you will learn to –

**Creature** (*angrily*) De Lacey! All the time you say that you don't know – but you do know! Why do you grasp everything, and I nothing? Why must I learn it all, when it flies to you on the wind? – I am the one who stands outside the door. I see inside. But I daren't go in.

**De Lacey** What is it exactly that frightens you?

**Creature** Everything! Everything! – Why do you live in a hut in the woods? Why not a great city?

**De Lacey** Because I'm poor.

**Creature** Why?

**De Lacey** Because an army came by, and they ransacked my university. And we were driven from the town.

**Creature** Am I poor?

**De Lacey** Yes. One day, though, you will find someone who will make you the wealthiest man in creation.

**Creature** Will I?

**De Lacey** Yes! A good man deserves it. You are a good man. Someone will love you, whoever you are.

**Creature** What is love?

### SCENE NINETEEN

*A dream: the plains of Argentina. Hot blue sky and lush grass. A Female Creature, constructed like the male, but physically very beautiful, sleeps in a nest in the grass.*
  *The Creature enters, and kneels lovingly by her.*

**Creature**
  'Awake, my fairest, my espoused, my latest found,
  Heaven's last best gift, my ever new delight,
  Awake!'

*She wakes. The Creature raises her to her feet. Music plays, and the female dances.*
  *It's a dance unlike anything you might have seen before.*

*Summer. De Lacey's cottage. He and the Creature are at the table. The Creature has Frankenstein's journal open in front of him.*

**Creature** I ran from a building. It was dark. I was frightened.

**De Lacey** Is that all you can remember?

**Creature** I do not know how to remember.

**De Lacey** But you have a memory, you have remembrance –

**Creature** But how is it done? What is the process?

**De Lacey** I don't know how it's done!

**Creature** Then how am I doing it?

**De Lacey** I do not know! You ran from a building? And this was in Ingolstadt? But the author of this journal says he's from –

**Creature** Geneva. He says he's from Geneva. (*Reads from the front page.*) 'Victor Frankenstein, citizen of Geneva –'

**De Lacey** Frankenstein?

*He shakes his head.*

**Creature** Where is Geneva?

**De Lacey** To the south and west, many days' ride. Read on.

**Creature** 'Preparing a frame for the experiment, with all its intricacies of fibres, muscles and veins, is a work of great difficulty. Should I attempt the creation of a being like myself, or one of simpler organisation?'

**De Lacey** 'A being like myself'? Meaning what? A man, a woman?

**Creature** De Lacey – I see things in my sleep!

**De Lacey** They are called dreams. What did you see?

**Creature** Someone! Her hair was long . . . and her eyes were –

**De Lacey** It was a good dream?

**Creature** It was pleasing! Is that good?

**De Lacey** A good dream doesn't mean it was morally good. It only means it wasn't a bad dream.

**Creature** (*worried*) There are bad dreams?

*Felix and Agatha are approaching the cottage. Agatha is heavily pregnant.*

**Agatha** (*calls*) Hello!

**Felix** Father!

**De Lacey** It's Felix and Agatha. Stay and meet them.

**Creature** No, I cannot!

**De Lacey** These are good people, they are not like the others! I don't know what you look like, my friend, but I know there is room in the world for fellowship, room in the world for love! Prejudice can be overcome! Stay! I will speak for you!

*The Creature stuffs the journal into his pocket. He looks for an escape route.*

**Felix** (*outside*) We're back!

**Agatha** (*outside*) Finished for today!

**De Lacey** I'm here! (*To the Creature.*) Hold my hand.

**Creature** I must run!

**De Lacey** No, trust me! Trust me! Stay here – stay!

**Creature** They will hate me!

**De Lacey** No, I promise you, no!

*The Creature is now trapped. De Lacey holds his hand. Felix comes in first, bearing armfuls of produce from the fields.*

**Felix** Father!

**De Lacey** This is my friend, he –

*Felix is speechless at the sight of the Creature. He drops his vegetables.*

**Creature** Good day, sir.

*For a moment they remain still, as if spellbound. Then Agatha enters. She immediately screams at the sight of the Creature.*

**Agatha** (*screams*) What is it?

**Felix** Get away from him! You! Get away!

*The Creature tries to run, but De Lacey holds on tight.*

**Creature** Gnaaaaagh!

**Felix** Let him go, you devil!

**De Lacey** Stay!

**Agatha** Felix!

*Felix takes a whip from his belt.*

**Felix** Leave my father be!

**De Lacey** No, no – there's nothing wrong!

27

**Agatha** Aah, it's revolting!

**Felix** Get out! Get out! Out!

*Felix lashes the Creature, who cowers under his blows.*

**Agatha** Drive it out!

**De Lacey** No! Felix! He's –

**Agatha** Thrash it! Thrash it! Kill it!

**Creature** (*to De Lacey*) You promised!

*The Creature is driven out. He runs away. De Lacey has been thrown to the floor.*

**Agatha** Awful, awful beast! – Are you hurt?

**Felix** (*helping De Lacey up*) You're safe – we shan't leave you again –

**De Lacey** (*angrily*) He was hungry! He did me no harm! Have you no compassion?

**Felix** It was a monster!

**De Lacey** No man is a monster!

**Agatha** But it wasn't a man!

**De Lacey** What have I done? Dear God, what have I done?

## SCENE TWENTY-ONE

*The Creature enters carrying aloft a blazing firebrand. He dances a war dance. His anger makes him inarticulate.*

**Creature** Ugh ggrr ugh! Wayaargh! Wayaargh!

*He approaches De Lacey's cottage.*

What do they do when they feel like this?
Heroes, Romans – what do they do?
I know.
They plot.
They revenge.

*He sets fire to the cottage. A wall of flame springs up.*

I sweep to my revenge!

*De Lacey, Felix and Agatha are consumed by the flames. They scream for help. The Creature backs away. The cottagers burn.*

### SCENE TWENTY-TWO

*By the shore of a lake. Snow-capped mountains in the distance. Several women enter at a run. They are Elizabeth Lavenza, twenties, her maid Clarice, and housemaids.*

**Elizabeth** Hide! Hide!

*They run and hide, giggling. All exit as William, a young boy, enters. He wears a sailor suit with a hat. He has the heels of his hands pushed into his eyes and is spinning round and counting.*

**William** Twenty-four, twenty-five, twenty-six . . . Get ready, everyone! Twenty-seven, twenty-eight, twenty-nine, twenty-nine and a half – thirty! Ready or not, I'm coming! (*He staggers.*) Oops, I'm giddy! (*He laughs.*) You'd better be well hidden!

*The Creature has entered behind William.*

**Creature** Hello. Boy.

**William**  Yes, sir?

*William starts to turn around.*

**Creature**  No! Don't turn around.

**William**  What?

**Creature**  I said don't turn around! Please don't!

**William**  Very well, sir.

**Creature**  Where am I?

**William**  Near Geneva.

**Creature**  Geneva?

**William**  Yes, sir. The lake – can't you see it? It's there!

*The Creature sees the lake and is pleased.*

**Creature**  The lake. How it glistens! – I've come a long way. Walking at night. Fish in the streams. Do you fish?

**William**  Oh, yes!

**Creature**  What do you catch? What bait do you use?

**William**  I should go to my friends. We're playing!

*The Creature steals up behind William and holds him tight.*

**Creature**  Guess who I am.

**William**  Are you a friend of the family's?

**Creature**  Yes.

**William**  Then you're a judge, or a minister, perhaps.

**Creature**  I am a judge.

*William tries to turn around.*

Don't look!

**William**  What?

**Creature** Don't look at me!

**William** I shan't.

**Creature** What's your name?

**William** William. What's yours, sir?

**Creature** You can be my friend, William. We could go hiking. We could climb those mountains over there!

**William** Climb Mont Blanc?

**Creature** Yes!

**William** Great!

**Creature** Let's go, friend!

**William** No, I'm not allowed. Sorry. Father would be angry.

**Creature** Forget him. Come with me. Let's climb Mont Blanc!

**William** I'd like to, but I can't!

**Creature** We must be friends. Everyone has friends.

**William** I have to find my father! Let me go! Let me go!

*William struggles.*

**Creature** I will release you if you answer my question.

**William** What is it?

**Creature** I seek a man called Frankenstein. Have you heard of him?

**William** That's my name!

**Creature** You? Frankenstein?

*Suddenly very curious, the Creature lets William go. William turns, looks, and yells.*

31

**William** Aargh! You're ugly! Leave me alone!

*William tries to run, but the Creature catches him.*

**Creature** Victor Frankenstein? He is your father?

**William** No! Victor's my brother!

**Creature** Where is he?

**William** He's at home, he's always at home –

**Creature** Can I see him?

**William** No, of course you can't!

**Creature** We must be friends, William. We'll climb those mountains. Right to the top. After you take me to Victor.

**William** No! You're revolting!

**Creature** What is he? What does he do?

**William** He's a scholar, a genius!

**Creature** Was he ever in Ingolstadt?

**William** Yes, he studied there, he's come home to marry Elizabeth, but he's silly, he never leaves his room! He's missing everything!

**Creature** You will bring him to me. Come.

**William** No! I shan't!

**Creature** Come.

*The Creature picks up the struggling William.*

**William** My father's a magistrate! He'll punish you for this. You'll go to prison! Help!

**Creature** Quiet, boy.

*The Creature gags him. He makes off towards the mountains.*

*The same place, some time later. It's now night. Servants of the Frankenstein household enter, searching. They carry flaming torches.*

**Servants** William! William!

*They are joined by Monsieur Frankenstein, Victor's father, and Elizabeth and Clarice.*

**M. Frankenstein** This is where you were playing?

**Elizabeth** (*tearfully*) Yes, we were hiding, he was coming to find us and –

**M. Frankenstein** Where were you hiding?

**Elizabeth** Down at the boat house.

**M. Frankenstein** You didn't see anything?

**Elizabeth** No, nothing!

**M. Frankenstein** And heard nothing?

**Elizabeth** He was calling out – I thought it was part of the game! Oh, what has happened to him?

*Victor enters. He looks in bad shape – ragged and unkempt.*

**Victor** William! William! – Divide into teams! You and you – come with me!

**M. Frankenstein** They are looking. Everyone is looking. You may go home.

**Victor** But William's missing! How long has it been?

**M. Frankenstein** Since this afternoon. But you may go home.

**Victor** I've a duty to help.

**M. Frankenstein** Victor, it doesn't help anybody when you become agitated –

**Victor** He's my brother! Let me join the search! I must!

**M. Frankenstein** (*sighs*) Very well, stay. But please – keep close to me.

**Victor** Why?

**Servants** Over here! Monsieur Frankenstein! Look at this!

*They have found William's sailor hat. All go towards it.*

**M. Frankenstein** It's William's hat.

**Victor** What was he doing here?

**Elizabeth** We were playing hide-and-seek.

**Victor** And you didn't keep him in view?

**Elizabeth** I was hiding from him! How could I keep him in view?

**Victor** But where were you?

**Elizabeth** Well, where were you? Locked in your study, I suppose?

**Victor** William was not my responsibility, he was yours!

**Elizabeth** So you have responsibility for – what, exactly?

**M. Frankenstein** Enough! The villagers are saying – Clarice?

*Clarice steps forward.*

**Clarice** They say they've seen a beast in the mountains, sir.

**Victor** A beast? What kind of a beast?

**Servant 1** A monster! Tall as a pine tree!

**Servant 2** They say it breathes blue fire!

**M. Frankenstein** They think this thing took William?

**Clarice** Well, someone took him! He's not to be found.

**Servant 1** No one knows what's up those mountains.

**Clarice** I know what's up those mountains. Snow and ice. And a bit more snow and ice. That's all!

**M. Frankenstein** Spread out! Keep looking! He may be nearby.

*They search. Victor is left with Elizabeth.*

**Victor** What do they mean – a monster?

**Elizabeth** They've seen some kind of animal, presumably.

**Victor** They didn't say an animal, they said a monster, a creature –

**Elizabeth** Folk tales!

**Victor** Who exactly saw it?

**Elizabeth** I don't know! Does it matter?

**Victor** This is dreadful.

**Elizabeth** Victor, you don't look well. I haven't seen you for weeks. You're always up in your room.

**Victor** Why do you need to see me?

**Elizabeth** We're supposed to be getting married!

**Victor** Oh, so I'm expected to –

**Elizabeth** – talk to me occasionally, yes!

**Victor** But what if I haven't got anything to say? What am I meant to do then?

35

*Servants call to M. Frankenstein.*

**Servants** Monsieur! Come and see! On the lake!

*Everyone runs to the shore.*

**M. Frankenstein** What is it?

**Servant 1** An open boat! But see – it's drifting against the current!

**Elizabeth** That's impossible!

**Servant 2** Against the wind!

**Elizabeth** Is someone pulling it?

**Servant 2** No, no one!

**Victor** Is there anyone aboard?

**M. Frankenstein** Haul it in!

*The Servants wade into the lake and drag a small boat back on to the shore. Everyone runs to it. Victor climbs in.*

**Victor** William!

**Clarice** Is it the child?

**Elizabeth** Oh, please, no!

*Victor lifts William's lifeless body from the boat. Papers torn from Victor's journal flutter from the body – diagrams and equations.*

**Victor** He's dead, Father.

**M. Frankenstein** Is it him?

**Clarice** Angels in heaven! Little William! Have mercy on his soul!

**M. Frankenstein** My boy. Give me my boy.

*Victor passes William into his father's arms. Clarice prays. Elizabeth is studying the journal pages.*

**Elizabeth** What are these papers? Victor? It looks like your hand.

**M. Frankenstein** Let me see. (*To Victor.*) Why, they are yours!

**Elizabeth** Victor?

**M. Frankenstein** These are diagrams. Equations. University work! What are they doing here?

**Victor** It seems – they're from my journal –

**Elizabeth** Well, where's your journal?

**Victor** I don't know! I lost it! I don't know where it is!

*Victor suddenly turns and runs out. Elizabeth makes to go after him.*

**M. Frankenstein** Let him go, Elizabeth. Let him go.

**Clarice** (*aside to Servants*) Some say he's gifted. I say he's touched.

**M. Frankenstein** Sound the bell! My son is dead.

*He bears off William's body and all exit. The church bell tolls.*

### SCENE TWENTY-FOUR

*Victor ascends Mont Blanc. A snowy wasteland, high in the Alps.*

**Victor** Are you here? Where are you? Are you here?

*His cape billows in the howling wind. He has a stout stick.*

Where are you? Show yourself, you monstrous thing!

*There is a sound like a great exhalation of breath, as the glacier shudders and shifts.*
*Through the snowstorm the Creature is suddenly visible, standing very still on the ice. He makes a great leap towards Victor.*

My God! Muscular coordination – hand and eye – excellent tissue – perfect balance! And the sutures have held! I failed to make it handsome, but I gave it strength and grace.

*Victor circles the Creature. The Creature swivels to keep an eye on him.*

What an achievement! Unsurpassed in scientific endeavour! God, the madness of that night – the heat, the sweat, the infusions, the moment when I saw it crawl towards me, and I – and I –

**Creature** You ran away.

**Victor** What?

**Creature** You abandoned me.

**Victor** (*stunned*) It speaks!

**Creature** Yes, Frankenstein. It speaks.

**Victor** You know my name?

*The Creature hands Victor the tattered journal.*

My journal!

**Creature** Why did you abandon me?

**Victor** I was terrified – what had I done?

**Creature** Built a man, and given him life –

**Victor** Well, now I have come to take it away –

38

**Creature** (*laughs*) Oh, have you?

**Victor** I have come to kill you!

**Creature** To kill me? Why then did you create me?

**Victor** To prove that I could!

**Creature** So you make sport with my life?

**Victor** In the cause of science! You were my greatest experiment – but an experiment that has gone wrong. An experiment that must be curtailed!

*Victor runs at him and attacks him with his stick, but the Creature swiftly disarms him and throws him to the ground.*

**Creature** Be still, genius! I have a request.

**Victor** Damn you, you can't have requests!

**Creature** Oh, I can! Listen to me. It's your duty.

**Victor** I've no duty to a murderer.

**Creature** If I'm a murderer, you made me one.

**Victor** You killed my brother! You did it, not me! – I curse the day when you drew breath. Since then I've lived in darkness.

**Creature**
'Is this the region, this the soil, the clime,
Said then the lost Archangel, this the seat
That we must change for Heaven, this mournful gloom
For that celestial light?'

**Victor** (*astonished*) That's *Paradise Lost*! You've read *Paradise Lost*?

**Creature** I liked it.

**Victor** Why? You saw yourself as Adam?

**Creature** I should be Adam. God was proud of Adam. But Satan's the one I sympathise with. For I was cast out, like Satan, though I did no wrong. And when I see others content, I feel the bile rise in my throat, and it tastes like Satan's bile.

**Victor** But this is remarkable! You are educated! And you have memory!

**Creature** Yes, I use it to remember being hunted like a rat, running from human places, finding refuge in the woods. I use it to remember being beaten and whipped. And I was good, I wanted to be good!

**Victor** Then why did you kill William?

**Creature** I wished to see you, and you came. Would you have come otherwise? If I had killed half of Ingolstadt, would you have come?

**Victor** (*subdued*) Did no one show you kindness?

**Creature** There was an old man. He taught me many things. But he was blind, he never saw my face. He never knew I looked like this! After a year, after he'd described to me the seasons, and I'd watched them go round, one, two, three, four – when I was one year old, he said they'd take me in. The son, and his wife. A beautiful wife.

**Victor** What happened?

**Creature** You know what happened.

**Victor** Oh, God, I do.

**Creature** I burned them. In a fire.

**Victor** Do you feel no remorse?

**Creature** Remorse? When I walk through a village, the children throw stones. When I beg for food, they loose their dogs. What is the function of remorse?

**Victor** I'm sorry, I –

**Creature** Sorry? You're sorry? You caused this! This is your universe!

*Victor is silent.*

Frankenstein. Here is my request. I wish to be part of society. But no human being will associate with me. But one of my own kind – one just as deformed and horrible – she would understand – she would –

**Victor** What, I –

**Creature** I want a female. Built like me.

**Victor** A female?

**Creature** You alone have the power to –

**Victor** Create another brute – another monster? No, I will not, I –

**Creature** It is my right!

**Victor** You have no rights. You are a slave. You want me to make you a female, so the pair of you can be wicked together? No, I will not. Torture me as much as you like, I'll never consent!

**Creature** I will not torture you. I will reason with you. Isn't that what we do? Have a dialogue?

**Victor** There is no dialogue with killers!

**Creature** Yet you'd kill me if you could! Why, you have just tried! So why is your killing justified, and mine is not?

**Victor** I won't argue with you! My God, I'm halfway up a mountain, debating with a – a –

**Creature** A living creature!

**Victor** A nothing, a filthy mass of nothing! I am your master, and you should show respect –

**Creature** A master has duties – you left me to die! I am not a slave. I am free. If you deny my request I will make you my enemy, I will work at your destruction, I will dedicate myself, I won't rest until I desolate your heart! (*Pause.*) I apologise. I did intend to reason. I am capable of logic. I do not think what I ask is immoderate? A creature of another sex, but as hideous as I am. If you consent, we'll disappear for ever. We'll go to the wilds of South America, and we'll build our little paradise, and live there in peace. And no human being will see us again. What do you say?

**Victor** I am amazed. You've learnt so much, so fast!

**Creature** Are you proud of me?

**Victor** Proud? No.

**Creature** Why not?

**Victor** Because your logic is flawed.

**Creature** Is it?

**Victor** You say you'll go abroad and disappear, yet you also say you yearn to be accepted by society. But won't you grow tired of exile? Won't you return, and try once more to live among people, only to meet with their detestation? Because that is what you will meet with. But now, when you run wild, there will be two of you, and double the destruction. Why should I facilitate this?

**Creature** Because I am lonely! Every creature has a mate. Every bird in the sky! Even you are to be married! Why am I denied the comforts you allow yourself? A moment ago you were amazed at my intellect, but now you harden your heart. Please, do not be inconsistent, I find it infuriating! All I ask is the possibility of love.

**Victor** Love?

**Creature** Yes!

**Victor** You think it is a possibility?

**Creature** Yes!

**Victor** For you?

**Creature** A good man deserves it!

**Victor** Are you a good man?

**Creature** I would be! Oh, I would be!

**Victor** I regret that you are lonely. I did not foresee –

**Creature** That I might have feelings?

**Victor** You were an equation. A theorem. I confess it. A puzzle to be solved. But if you are – sentient – and if you will – depart –

**Creature** Frankenstein, if you give me a companion, I will quit Europe for ever, I will vanish into air. There will be no more destruction. I will be gone.

*A pause. Victor thinks.*

**Victor** Will you swear to be peaceful?

**Creature** Yes! I beg you to believe me!

**Victor** If you gave me your word that you'd leave here for ever, and never return – never! If you were to swear, and swear solemnly –

**Creature** I swear by the blue sky, by the white snow, by the fire of love that burns in my heart, that if you grant my request, you will never have to look on me again, for as long as the world turns round!

**Victor** You think it turns round?

**Creature** Well, of course.

**Victor** You must understand – the work is hard –

**Creature** You alone can do it. You alone have the skill.

**Victor** I alone – in the whole world – and no one to share the secret! – Look, down there. (*He points down the mountain.*) Do you see them? Little men, with little lives.

**Creature** (*excited*) Little houses! Little men!

**Victor** Pygmies. I am different.

**Creature** You are a king! The King of Science! Build me a woman. Please! A bride.

**Victor** A bride should be beautiful. A bride should have pretty eyes, and shining hair. She should not be hideous. She should be as lovely as possible.

**Creature** Oh yes!

**Victor** I will not repeat my mistakes. We can only go forward. We can never go back.

**Creature** Master, work your magic once more, I beg you!

**Victor** (*thinking*) A female . . . I haven't ever considered the question. There are differences of anatomy, of course, but also differences of – what? – temperament? Humour? Skill?

**Creature** (*happily*) I don't know!

**Victor** What are females good at?

**Creature** I don't know!

*Victor is not really listening.*

**Victor** My God, what a challenge! If I could make something immaculate, something that I could – exhibit? Not a demon but a – a goddess!

44

**Creature** A goddess.

**Victor** Yes! If she was – indistinguishable from a – if she was perfect! Imagine that! – I may be damned but I'll attempt it.

**Creature** You will comply with my request?

**Victor** I will comply with your request. If you give me your word that, afterward – you will leave us be.

**Creature** I will! If you give me your word that you will do it!

*Victor holds out his hand.*

What is that for?

**Victor** You shake it.

**Creature** I shake it?

**Victor** We seal the bargain. Take my hand.

*Tentatively, the Creature takes Victor's hand. They shake.*

**Creature** Thank you! Thank you! My dreams come true! Go home and begin at once!

**Victor** At home? I can't do it at home!

**Creature** Why not? What happens at home?

**Victor** Do this work in my father's house? No!

**Creature** Then go where you need to. I will be watching!

*The Creature swiftly clambers away over the ice cliff, sure-footed like a goat. As Victor watches him go, we once again hear the breath of the glacier.*

*The Frankenstein house, Geneva. Clarice, in mourning blacks, brings Monsieur Frankenstein his post on a tray.*

**Clarice** Your post, sir.

**M. Frankenstein** (*taking it, sadly*) Letters of condolence.

**Clarice** The Lord giveth, and the Lord taketh away.

**M. Frankenstein** I know, Clarice. I know.

*Victor bursts into the room. He has come straight from his encounter with the Creature, and still wears his furs and boots. In his hand he clutches the journal.*

**Victor** (*to Clarice*) Out.

*Clarice exits.*

**M. Frankenstein** Victor! Where have you been?

**Victor** In the mountains, on the Sea of Ice.

**M. Frankenstein** This is a house of death. It is no time to go adventuring!

**Victor** Father – I have to make a long journey. I leave today.

**M. Frankenstein** Today! But what about William?

**Victor** He isn't coming. I must travel to England. Goodbye.

**M. Frankenstein** England? Why?

**Victor** Work.

**M. Frankenstein** What work? For a year I have not seen you work! What is this work for which you must decamp to England?

**Victor** Look, I don't expect you to understand, but –

**M. Frankenstein** No, I do not understand! I do not believe your studies are so important, and I order you to remain here for the funeral!

**Victor** I have no intention of obeying. I must go.

**M. Frankenstein** And your wedding?

**Victor** It will have to be postponed.

**M. Frankenstein** But Elizabeth –

**Victor** Elizabeth will wait. I was in Ingolstadt six years. A little longer won't make much difference.

**M. Frankenstein** Victor, why are you so sad?

*Victor is silent.*

When your mother was dying –

**Victor** Please don't bring her into it –

**M. Frankenstein** When your mother was dying, I gave a promise that I would see you wed your cousin Elizabeth. That was my wife's last wish – that you might be happily married. You were such a sunny child, a carefree child, alert and inquisitive, the joy of our days! I came to believe you would do great things, and I would be proud of you! Instead we have this sullenness, this melancholy, this low fog of gloom. You flout my authority; you do not respect the codes by which we live. In short, you disappoint me. If you insist on leaving, I cannot stop you. But you may tell your fiancée yourself. (*Calls off.*) Elizabeth? (*He turns back.*) Where is the boy I remember? He had bright eyes and a ready smile. Where is he, Victor? Where has he gone?

*M. Frankenstein exits. Victor waits. He hears again, distantly, the terrifying breath of the glacier. Victor senses that the Creature is observing.*

*Elizabeth enters.*

**Elizabeth** Your father tells me you are leaving us. Why, Victor? Why must you go to England?

**Victor** Because in England they are at the forefront of electro-chemistry. I've heard of real breakthroughs by vitalists, galvanists. I must go and see for myself!

**Elizabeth** And for that, you'll put off our wedding?

**Victor** Yes! It's critical for my experiments.

**Elizabeth** What are your experiments?

**Victor** I'd say they're beyond a woman's scope.

**Elizabeth** If you think I'm going to marry someone who talks to me like that, you can think again. Which part might be beyond my scope?

**Victor** All of it, actually.

**Elizabeth** Are you suggesting I'm less intelligent than you?

**Victor** Yes. I mean – less educated.

**Elizabeth** That's hardly my fault. I wasn't allowed to go to school! But I can learn. I could be your assistant.

**Victor** What is a Voltaic pile? A Leyden jar? Electric eggs?

**Elizabeth** You know perfectly well I don't know. What is a voltaic pile?

**Victor** It's for storing an electrostatic charge. You link several jars in parallel, and with that you can –

**Elizabeth** Oh, please, take me with you! It sounds so exciting!

**Victor** I will go first to Oxford, and spend several months at the University. Believe me, there's nothing exciting about that.

**Elizabeth** I don't care! I'll come.

**Victor** I'll be in the library all day.

**Elizabeth** I'll be as quiet as a mouse. Let me come!

**Victor** Subsequently I'll travel to the islands of Scotland – barren rocks in a barren ocean. It is, I am told, an awful place.

**Elizabeth** I don't care! We'll be together!

**Victor** Elizabeth – it's no situation for a woman –

**Elizabeth** What, and you think this is? The world is turning, and I'm sitting in Switzerland, watching it! I know it's picturesque, the mountains, the lake, but it's so quiet it's oppressive, and the people are dull. I want to go to Paris, Rome, America! I want to talk to you about your work, about the world, about music, politics, everything!

**Victor** I have no interest in music or politics.

**Elizabeth** Have you any interest in me? (*Pause.*) Victor, are you hiding something?

**Victor** No!

**Elizabeth** But there is something on your mind – and I believe I know what it is. I believe I know what obsesses you.

**Victor** (*alarmed*) Do you?

**Elizabeth** Yes, you have given too many hints, that you –

**Victor** What? That I what?

**Elizabeth** That there's someone else.

*Victor is fearful.*

Victor, is there a girl in Ingolstadt? Are you in love with someone else?

**Victor** No, no! I'm not in love with anyone else!

**Elizabeth** But you are constantly preoccupied, as if you are yearning to be with someone else –

**Victor** No, it's you, Elizabeth, it's always been you! There's no one else. I promise!

**Elizabeth** (*relieved*) Oh, Victor! I've been so alone, I've been lonelier since you returned than when you were away! I see a rainbow or a sunset and I long to share it, but you're not with me, you're never with me, there's only one where there should be two. All I ask is to come with you, and be at the centre of things. I want your gravity, your volume, your mass – not an abstract – you.

**Victor** I'm sorry. It's impossible. I must go alone.

**Elizabeth** Victor, what do you think love is?

**Victor** I'll be back in six months.

**Elizabeth** That wasn't much of answer.

**Victor** Well, it's not quantifiable, is it? I mean, what do you measure? The number of kisses?

**Elizabeth** You don't measure anything. You throw yourself in. It's like jumping from the rocks into a swirling pool – you throw yourself in – you drown. You drown in love!

**Victor** I see. You drown.

**Elizabeth** May I ask you something? I want to have children. Do you want to have children?

**Victor** Yes, of course, I –

**Elizabeth** Do you want to give me children?

**Victor** God willing. Yes I do.

**Elizabeth** I've waited and waited.

**Victor** It will soon be over. Just let me finish my work. If only I could tell someone about it!

**Elizabeth** Tell me, please, tell me!

**Victor** I can't, I can't tell anyone! I wish I could tell you, but I can't!

**Elizabeth** Then just kiss me. Like this.

*She kisses him hard, and fondles him.*

(*Whispers.*) Show me how you'll give me children. Touch me. Feel my heat!

*She places his hands on her body.*

Must you go? Must you? Can't you stay?

**Victor** If only I could stay . . .! But I cannot.

**Elizabeth** Then go, and do your work, and be brilliant! And after that come home to me, and be my husband, and give me a dozen children!

*Victor steps back and appraises her very thoroughly.*

**Victor** You are beautiful. You will make a beautiful wife.

**Elizabeth** Victor! What do you think I am, a specimen? – Go!

*Laughing, she pushes him towards the door.*

*Some weeks later. A tumbledown croft in the Orkneys.*
*The weather is appalling.*
    *Two crofters enter carrying a heavy trunk from a boat*
*to the croft. They are Ewan, an older man, and Rab,*
*younger. Victor follows them.*

**Victor** Is the weather always like this?

**Rab** This is quite a nice day.

**Ewan** It's not much of a croft, sir. The roof is poor. Will
you be all right here?

**Victor** For my needs, it's fine. Your wife can bring me
some food?

**Ewan** She can, sir, but it's simple. Fish, mainly. We don't
touch meat, do we, Rab? Unless it swims, we don't eat it.

**Rab** Eggs, we eat eggs.

**Ewan** That's the exception. Eggs.

**Rab** Oatcakes. Turnips.

**Ewan** (*glaring at Rab*) All right! – Where do you want
it, sir?

    *They enter the croft.*

**Victor** Set it down there. Thank you, gentlemen. Here's
the price we agreed, for the porterage and three months'
rent.

    *Victor lays down money. Ewan goes to pick it up, but*
    *Victor stops him.*

But I would be prepared to give you very much more,
Ewan, if you could perform another service for me.
(*Beat.*) My field, you see, is human anatomy. The human

body. To progress my research, I require certain materials. This is an unorthodox discipline, and somewhat disapproved of in academic circles. But you have my word that it is for the public good.

*Victor takes off his travelling cloak. He opens the trunk and, as they talk, he sets out on the table various surgical instruments, particularly saws and knives; galvanic batteries and coils of wire; Voltaic pile, etc.*

**Rab** I don't like the sound of that.

**Ewan** Quiet, Rab. We don't move in academic circles. (*To Victor.*) Go on, sir. It's illegal, I take it?

**Victor** We are a long way from any court of law. The nights are dark. And in science we keep our secrets.

**Ewan** What is it you want?

**Victor** Body parts. Fresh.

**Rab** He's a surgeon! I knew it! That's grave-robbing!

**Ewan** We are Christians in the Orkneys, sir. We don't rob the dead in their graves.

**Victor** But the dead are dead, aren't they? They're not coming back. I don't subscribe to the view that it's unethical to use them for medical research.

**Ewan** No, nor do we.

**Victor** What will be possible in the future, eh, Rab? Shall we gain the upper hand over sickness and disease? Have you any idea what we shall be capable of, if brilliant men are allowed to do our work?

**Rab** Uncle Ewan, this is not right –

**Ewan** Quiet, Rab! – I'll do nothing on my own island. But what is it exactly that you're after?

**Victor** Have you heard of any young woman who has died very recently?

**Ewan** (*thinks*) Aye. On Ronaldsay.

**Victor** Not your kin?

**Ewan** No, not my kin.

**Victor** Not diseased?

**Ewan** Drowned.

**Victor** May God have mercy on her.

**Ewan** A good-looking miss, she was. Rab liked her.

**Rab** I did not.

**Ewan** You did.

**Rab** I liked her sister.

**Victor** She was beautiful?

**Rab** Not bad.

**Victor** Good. Are you prepared to work to my exact specifications?

**Ewan** Well, Rab, he can't read, but –

**Rab** I can read.

**Ewan** Do him a drawing.

**Rab** Uncle Ewan –

*Ewan takes the money.*

**Ewan** You, be quiet, and do as the gentleman says!

**Victor** How far is it to Ronaldsay?

## SCENE TWENTY-SEVEN

*The Orkneys. Night. A graveyard. Wind and rain.*
*Ewan and Rab have dug up a grave. They are inside it,*
*forcing a corpse into a hessian sack. It's not easy work.*

**Ewan** Is she in?

**Rab** There's a bit sticking out.

**Ewan** What is it?

**Rab** I don't know, it's a girl.

**Ewan** Come on – push, laddie!

*They succeed in tying the sack.*

She's in!

*They rest.*

You have strange taste, Rab, that's all I can say. I find
her terribly skinny.

**Rab** I said the sister. The sister is fatter. (*Darkly.*) Uncle
Ewan, what's he going to do?

**Ewan** I don't know.

**Rab** This is not right, Uncle Ewan.

**Ewan** As the man said, they're dead. They're not coming
back. Ready?

**Rab** Yes.

**Ewan** Heave!

*They pull the sack up out of the grave. Victor enters,*
*in an oilskin, with a storm lantern.*

**Victor** Have you got it?

**Ewan** Aye, sir.

**Victor** Haul it to the boat. This is only the first, Ewan.

**Ewan** Is it, sir?

**Victor** I shall need a regular supply of internal organs.

**Ewan** Very good, sir.

**Rab** Organs!

**Ewan** Quiet, Rab. Meat for the dogs. Nothing you're not familiar with.

*They exit, dragging the sack. The Creature emerges from hiding. He is soaking wet from the rain, but untroubled by it.*

**Creature** Was this how I was formed?

*He approaches the grave.*

Stolen at night from wet soil? Made out of meat for the dogs? Even I can feel disgust! Will he fashion me a beauty, from this filth? And will I want her, stinking of death? (*Beat.*) I hunger for knowledge. But the more I learn, the less I understand. I feel stupid! A child! It was better when I knew nothing, when I had no questions, questions whirling like the wind! It was better when I howled in the woods!

### SCENE TWENTY-EIGHT

*The croft. Months later. Night. Victor is working on a Female Creature. Her body is complete and she is suspended upon a frame. Tools and instruments surround the grisly experiment, along with unused organs.*

*Victor wears his surgical apron. His eyes are bleary. He yawns.*

*There is a knock at the door, and Victor hastily covers the Female with a tarpaulin, and draws a curtain.*

**Victor** Come!

*Ewan enters, dragging a sack. The wind whips in, guttering the candles. The sack leaves a trail of blood and slime across the floor. Ewan deposits it by the work table.*

**Ewan** Here you are.

**Victor** Thank you, Ewan. That will be the last. Thank you for all your assistance.

**Ewan** You will be leaving our island soon?

**Victor** Soon.

**Ewan** Have we done you good service?

**Victor** Excellent service, yes.

**Ewan** And the food was all right?

**Victor** The food was unbelievable.

**Ewan** Sir – you're not looking too marvellous, if you don't mind my saying.

**Victor** I'm tired, that's all. But my work is nearly done! And let me tell you – I think I can say I have excelled.

**Ewan** I'm very pleased to hear it. Farewell to sickness and disease, eh?

*He tries to look behind the curtain but Victor prevents him.*

**Victor** Goodbye, Ewan.

**Ewan** Goodbye, sir.

*Ewan takes his money and leaves. Victor goes to the door and bolts it. Then he sits at the table. He doesn't*

*uncover the Female again, but puts his head on the*
*table and closes his eyes.*
   *There is movement in the sack.*
   *Out of the sack comes William, full of beans. Victor*
*opens his eyes. A dream:*

**Victor**  William

**William**  So how do you do it?

**Victor**  It's late, you should be in bed.

**William**  How do you bring dead things to life? Is it
easy?

**Victor**  No, it's hard. It's some kind of miracle.

**William**  Tell me the secret. When did you start?

**Victor**  At school.

**William**  Did you bring the teachers to life? That really
would be a miracle.

**Victor**  (*laughs*) School was so boring! I wanted to find
out why things exist – how things exist – not absurd
divinity, idiotic music. The laws of existence! So I began
to read forbidden books. Agrippa, Paracelsus.

**William**  The alchemists!

**Victor**  Yes! They were true men of science. They
mapped the heavens, tracked the course of the stars.
They classified the air we breathe, the circulation of our
blood. All modern medicine comes from them. – I too
wished to penetrate nature, to lay bare her deepest
mysteries. So I studied mathematics. I experimented with
galvanism –

**William**  What's that?

**Victor**  You induce spasms in inanimate flesh, with a
current from a chloride battery –

**William** Great!

**Victor** – where a zinc plate's laid on a solution of ammonium chloride and Ceylon moss –

**William** How thrilling!

**Victor** – and as I watched the current arc between bismuth and antimony, I found myself asking: where does the principle of life, the actual spark of life itself, where does it come from?

**William** It comes from God.

**Victor** Yes, but only from God?

**William** I don't know.

**Victor** Can a man be a god?

**William** I don't know!

**Victor** I had to find out. I believed that to examine the causes of life, one had to begin with death. So I went to dissections, but they were too clinical, too after-the-fact. I had to see at first hand the process of decay. So off to the graveyard I went.

**William** Oh, Victor! Yuk!

**Victor** I watched flesh rot in the soil. I watched worms eat eyes, maggots chew the tissue of the brain. I went to executions, charnel houses, I watched the moment of change from life to death, the specificity of the moment, the annihilation of the spark, until suddenly, months later, in a fever of creativity, I found I could identify and replicate the prime cause of life!

**William** (*excited*) What is it?

**Victor** I can't tell you that, Will, you're only little.

**William** What are you going to do with it?

**Victor** I don't know. I have travelled where no man has travelled. I wonder how far I can go. I can create people, Will! Living people! Look at me, I breathe the breath of God!

**William** And will they reproduce?

**Victor** What?

**William** Will they have wombs, the females? Will they breed? How quickly will they breed? How fast is the cycle? How many in a litter? Fifty? A hundred? A thousand?

**Victor** William?

**William** And if the children breed with the children? Will they do your bidding?

**Victor** What are you saying?

**William** You are their king – will they do as you tell them? Or will they be bad? Like the one who killed me?

**Creature** Frankenstein!

*The Creature is high up in the rafters. He's been there a while. William runs off. Victor wakes from his dream.*

Where is she?

**Victor** She is here.

*The Creature swings down to the ground.*

**Creature** Show me, genius!

**Victor** Wait.

*Victor goes behind the curtain and reappears with the Female. He steadies her as she walks under her own volition. She has minimal animation but apparently no mental function.*

**Creature**  Oh! Look!

*Victor supports the Female as the Creature's eyes widen with delight. He sinks to his knees before her.*

**Victor**  Isn't she fine?

**Creature**  Oh, she is beautiful!

**Victor**  Yes.

**Creature**  Your work is so detailed! The hairs on her arms – the curve of her hips!

*The Creature touches her gently. The Female makes a slight movement in response.*

**Victor**  She is perfect. A perfect wife.

**Creature**  Frankenstein, I admire you.

**Victor**  I can't give her to you.

**Creature**  Why not?

**Victor**  How do I know what will happen – if I bring her fully to life? I didn't know how you'd turn out – how dangerous you'd be – how can I know about her?

**Creature**  Sir. If it has been possible for me to overcome my disgusting origins, and transform myself into a rational being, she, my wife, can do the same.

**Victor**  And if she doesn't?

**Creature**  But she will. I will teach her morality, as De Lacey taught me –

**Victor**  But you have sworn to live as an outcast. Supposing she prefers the town?

**Creature**  She has no choice, we go to Argentina –

**Victor**  But what if she refuses to accept a bargain made before she was even created? Come on, use your brain.

She might reject you. She might abhor the sight of you! She might take one look at you and run – she might say she wants to live with a man, not a monster!

**Creature** Stop talking! You are cruel!

**Victor** But look at her! Look! Exquisitely constructed, don't you agree? Look at her cheeks, her lips, her breasts! Who would not desire those breasts? What if she leaves you? What if she finds someone else? How will you feel if you're deserted by one of your own species, the only one of your own species, the only one you can take to your bed – how will you react?

**Creature** I will run mad if she leaves me!

**Victor** It's a risk, then, isn't it?

**Creature** No, because I will give her such adoration, such devotion, she will never want to leave!

**Victor** So it is a risk I should take?

**Creature** You must! You must!

*He strokes her hair.*

She is mine. Please. Please.

**Victor** Are you saying you will protect her?

**Creature** Yes, oh yes. Nobody will harm her. I will be there.

**Victor** Are you saying you will love her?

**Creature** Yes, I am!

**Victor** Because love is not something one can teach, not something one can learn. Either you feel it in your soul, or –

**Creature** Oh, master! I do! I love her! I do!

**Victor** You're telling me you have a soul?

**Creature** I must! Say you believe me –

**Victor** How does it feel, to be in love?

**Creature** It feels like all the life is bubbling up in me and spilling from my mouth, it feels like my lungs are on fire and my heart is a hammer, it feels like I can do anything in the world! Anything in the world!

**Victor** Is that how it feels?

**Creature** Yes!

*A heartbreaking moment in which it becomes clear that the Creature may be more capable of love than Victor is.*

That is how it feels. Bring her to life, and I will cherish her for ever.

**Victor** Those are the words I was waiting to hear. You have shown me you have some grasp of the emotion we call love. Now, be patient. I will complete her.

*Victor leads the Female back behind the curtain.*

You can help me. We will not send her out into the world in this condition. We will dress her – dress her as a queen.

**Creature** A queen!

**Victor** Go to that trunk. It contains some clothes – my fiancée's. Select the finest, for your bride. – Now, let me work. I'll call you when you're needed.

*Victor exits with the Female. The Creature goes to the trunk, and opens the catches.*

**Creature** I'll clothe her in lace and velvet. I'll give her silks and pearls. I will walk in the garden with my fair angelic Eve! I will be Adam, she will be Eve! And all the memory of hell will melt like snow.

*The Creature pulls from the trunk a dusty book. And another. There are no clothes. He realises he's been tricked, and turns to hear an unpleasant noise. He tears aside the curtain to find that Victor is hacking up the Female with a cleaver. Victor scatters the limbs of the Female. She's utterly destroyed.*

Waargh!

**Victor** What do you know of the power of love? It is irrational, a pool of unreason! It is anarchic, volatile, vertiginous, mad! Above all it is uncontrollable! Millions of you on the earth? Coupling, procreating? No! You are the only one of your species – and that is how you will stay!

*The Creature sinks to his knees among the body parts.*

**Creature** Awake, my fairest, my espoused! Awake! Awake!

**Victor** She will never awake.

*The Creature grabs Victor by the throat. He begins to throttle him. There is a hammering at the door.*

**Constable** (*off*) Sir! Sir! Open the door!

**M. Frankenstein** (*off*) Victor! Let us in!

**Creature** Waaargh!

*The Creature dashes Victor to the floor and climbs to the window.*

Frankenstein – you broke your word – you may expect me again!

*The Creature exits. The hammering at the door continues.*

**M. Frankenstein** (*off*) Victor! Victor!

**Ewan** (*off*) There's something running off!

**Constable** (*off*) Jesus Christ! What is it?

**M. Frankenstein** Victor! Open the door!

*Monsieur Frankenstein, a Constable and Ewan burst in through the door. Victor collapses in his father's arms.*

**Victor** Father . . . ?

**Ewan** What in God's name is this place?

**Victor** Father . . . you came . . .

**M. Frankenstein** Victor, you were gone too long! We were worried!

**Victor** But you don't know what I've done!

**M. Frankenstein** You're safe, boy – I have come to take you home.

**Victor** Father, I must be married at once. I must marry Elizabeth! At once! At once!

**M. Frankenstein** Please, help me get him to the boat.

**Ewan** Aye, sir.

*They go to assist Victor. He breaks away and finds his journal, which he thrusts in M. Frankenstein's hands.*

**Victor** Take this. Take it! I want you to promise that you will destroy it!

**M. Frankenstein** Your journal?

**Victor** Destroy it, Father, burn it! No one must read it again! Will you give me your word, your word as a magistrate? That this will be destroyed?

**M. Frankenstein** I give you my word. Come home.

*M. Frankenstein leads Victor out of the croft.*

**Constable** What has he been doing here? You, man: speak.

**Ewan** Medical research, as he said, sir.

*The Constable surveys the bloody scene.*

**Constable** Medical research? Holy Christ!

*They exit.*

### SCENE TWENTY-NINE

*The Frankenstein house, by Lake Geneva.*
*Servants enter, celebrating with mugs of wine. They sing.*

**Servants**
The vows are sworn
The knot is tied
The garlands thrown
On groom and bride.

Lift up your voice
And raise your wine
To bless the house
Of Frankenstein.

*The Servants exit.*
*Elizabeth enters in her wedding dress, with Clarice. We're in the master bedroom; there is a large bed. They can hear wedding bells in the distance.*

**Clarice** Listen – you can still hear the bells ringing, over the water.

**Elizabeth** So you can.

*They listen for a moment.*

66

**Clarice** Many congratulations, Mistress. It was a splendid day.

**Elizabeth** Thank you. Please get me ready for bed.

**Clarice** Yes, Mistress.

*Clarice proceeds to help her undress.*

**Elizabeth** I want to look beautiful.

**Clarice** Yes, Mistress.

**Elizabeth** Perhaps then he'll –

**Clarice** I'm sure he will.

*Elizabeth breaks down and sobs.*

**Elizabeth** He never touches me! He never comes near! He barely spoke to me after the service!

**Clarice** Well, he has always been peculiar.

**Elizabeth** But what have I done wrong, Clarice?

**Clarice** You've done nothing, Mistress. Men, you know – they're as nervous as we are on their wedding night. A lot of them have no experience whatever.

**Elizabeth** I'm not nervous!

**Clarice** I know you're not, Mistress. And yet you don't know what to expect, do you? None of us do, first time. It can come as quite a shock. Here we are, Mistress – you'll look as pretty as a picture.

*Clarice helps her into a long nightgown, and unpins her hair.*

Some ladies never get used to it at all, to be perfectly honest. Oh, but I'm sure you will.

**Elizabeth** Where is he?

**Clarice** He'll be along shortly, Mistress. You wait and see. Having a glass or two, probably, if he's anything like my husband. He'd put a bag on my head if he could. Come along now, let's pop you into bed.

**Elizabeth** First I must pray. – That's all.

**Clarice** Goodnight, Mistress. God bless.

*Clarice curtsies and exits. Elizabeth kneels by her bed and prays. Victor enters. He has a pistol in each hand and a wild look on his face. After him come two Servants armed with muskets.*

**Elizabeth** Victor!

**Victor** Report!

**Servant 1** We patrol the terrace and the roof.

**Servant 2** We have men down at the lake.

**Victor** Good. Wait for me outside. I'll join you presently.

*The Servants exit. Victor hastily drinks a glass of spirits. Elizabeth is considerably alarmed.*

**Elizabeth** Victor, what is going on?

**Victor** The lodge is secured. There are guards at every door.

**Elizabeth** Why? What is going on? Tell me.

**Victor** I should have told you before.

**Elizabeth** Yes, I think you should!

**Victor** It is one of my experiments, Elizabeth. You will find this hard to credit, and there is little time to explain, but the simple fact is – I built a man.

**Elizabeth** You did what?

**Victor** I built a man. And succeeded in animating him.

**Elizabeth** Say that again?

**Victor** I built a man!

**Elizabeth** Animating him? Do you mean bringing him to life?

**Victor** Yes, bringing him to life – my creature, I brought him to life!

**Elizabeth** Your creature.

**Victor** You don't believe me.

**Elizabeth** Yes. Yes I do. If you say you have made a creature, and brought him to life, then – (*Solemnly.*) I do believe you, of course. (*She bursts out laughing.*) What is it, like a puppet?

**Victor** No, a functioning man – a brute of a man!

**Elizabeth** This is ridiculous. You are saying, you are telling me you have made some sort of creature, with your electric eggs presumably, and it – what? It does what?

**Victor** It pursues me.

**Elizabeth** Victor, you've been very ill. – In Scotland you – you had a nervous collapse.

**Victor** Look. There is a – a thing, out there – and it wants to destroy me! I have lured it here and now I must act – I must kill him before he kills me!

**Elizabeth** What do you mean, you have lured it here?

**Victor** I knew he would come for the – for the –

**Elizabeth** The wedding? Did you send him an invitation? Victor! He wasn't on the list!

**Victor** Elizabeth – this is serious! Please believe me!

**Elizabeth** You're asking me to believe that you have created some sort of monster?

**Victor** Yes, I –

**Elizabeth** Why?

**Victor** I beg your pardon?

**Elizabeth** Why? Why did you do that?

**Victor** Because I had a vision, a vision of perfection. I followed nature into her lair, and stripped her of her secrets. I brought torrents of light to a darkening world. I did it, Elizabeth, I did it!

**Elizabeth** I've never doubted your brilliance.

**Victor** I have beaten death! I have done it! I have made a living thing!

**Elizabeth** But if you wanted to create life –

**Victor** That's it, that's exactly what I wanted!

**Elizabeth** Why not just give me a child? We could have married years ago!

**Victor** No, no, that's not the –

**Elizabeth** Because that is how we create life, Victor – that is the usual way!

**Victor** I am talking about science –

**Elizabeth** No, you are talking about pride! You have been trying God's work – is that what you're telling me? And it has gone awry.

**Victor** In you I found paradise. But the apple is eaten. We cannot go back.

**Elizabeth** You've meddled with the natural order, and led us into chaos, because you worship the gods of electricity and gas! What is wrong with you men?

*Victor takes up his pistols.*

**Victor** I have guards all round the house. I will kill this thing that I foolishly made, and then I will come back to you.

**Elizabeth** Please, don't go, hold me! Please!

**Victor** Time for that when this is done. (*Earnestly.*) I will try to love you, Elizabeth.

**Elizabeth** Victor!

*Victor runs out. Elizabeth has her back to her bed. The Creature suddenly springs from inside it, and races towards her. He pins her arms behind her and clamps his hand over her mouth. She struggles, but he is too strong.*

**Creature** Don't scream! I will not hurt you. Don't scream! I need your help.

*Elizabeth struggles less. Still he pinions her.*

Can you guess who I am?

*Eyes wild with fright, Elizabeth nods.*

But he didn't mention what I look like, did he?

*Elizabeth shakes her head.*

Are you curious? Elizabeth?

*Slowly, despite her fear, she nods.*

Do not scream. I will release you.

*Carefully, he lets go of Elizabeth. She doesn't move.*

Turn around. Look at me.

*Elizabeth does so. She gasps.*

I need your help. I have a grievance.

**Elizabeth** Victor did this . . .?

**Creature** Do you think he's clever?

**Elizabeth** A genius!

**Creature** Oh yes, that's right!

*She peers at him with curiosity, going increasingly close.*

**Elizabeth** What's your name?

**Creature** My name? Oh, what luxury that would be! He didn't give me one. Touch.

*Elizabeth is scared. The Creature grasps her hand and puts it to his face.*

What do you feel, Elizabeth?

**Elizabeth** Heat.

*He places her hand over his heart.*

**Creature** Here?

**Elizabeth** A heartbeat.

**Creature** Just like yours.

*The Creature places his hand on Elizabeth's breast, and grins.*

**Elizabeth** (*sternly*) Now if you please – we'll have none of –

*Elizabeth looks him full in the eye, and he removes his hand.*

You say you have a grievance?

**Creature** Madame, your husband is a good man, but he does not keep his word. If you had a child, and it looked like me, would you abandon it?

72

**Elizabeth** I'd never abandon a child.

**Creature** Are you sure?

**Elizabeth** I'm sure.

**Creature** No matter how repulsive?

**Elizabeth** I'm sure!

**Creature** Well, he did. He left me. Because I look like this. Because I am different.

**Elizabeth** If Victor has treated you poorly, I shall speak to him. You may count on that.

**Creature** Isn't he coming to bed?

**Elizabeth** He must learn that he has to take responsibility for his actions, and that –

**Creature** Surely he desires you? On your wedding night?

**Elizabeth** – and that we must always stand up for the disadvantaged.

**Creature** Oh, absolutely, give voice to the oppressed. Will you put my case?

**Elizabeth** What is it you want?

**Creature** I did not ask to be born, but once born, I will fight to live. All life is precious – even mine. He promised to give me the only thing I lack, the only thing I need to be content, but then he broke his word. I want a friend! That's all!

**Elizabeth** (*tentatively*) I'll be your friend. If you'll let me.

**Creature** Will you?

**Elizabeth** If you need help, then . . . let's see what we can do.

**Creature** Sit with me. I will not hurt you, I promise. I am educated, I know right from wrong.

*She stares at him intently.*

**Elizabeth** Incredible. You are quite extraordinary, do you know that?

**Creature** Me?

**Elizabeth** Yes, you.

*He reaches out to take her hand. She takes it and he leads her to the bed. They sit side by side.*

**Creature** Perhaps I am a genius, too?

**Elizabeth** (*laughs*) Perhaps you are. What are you good at?

**Creature** I am good at the art of assimilation. I have watched, and listened, and learnt. At first I knew nothing at all. But I studied the ways of men, and slowly I learnt: how to ruin, how to hate, how to debase, how to humiliate. And at the feet of my master, I learnt the highest of human skills, the skill no other creature owns: I finally learnt how to lie.

**Elizabeth** Lie?

**Creature** Tonight I have met someone – perfect. Thank you for trying to understand. But he broke his promise; so I break mine. I am truly sorry, Elizabeth.

**Elizabeth** What do you –

*Elizabeth realises just too late. She bolts for the door, but he springs on her, again clamping his hand over her mouth. He drags her kicking back to the bed, where he rapes her. She kicks and struggles but to no avail. He forces apart her legs and enters her.*
*Victor runs in.*

*Victor hangs back in appalled fascination as he watches his Creature mating.*

*The Creature lets out an awful, agonised groan, and his hand slips from Elizabeth's mouth, and she screams.*

Victor!

**Victor** Elizabeth!

*The Creature looks up and sees Victor. Then he snaps Elizabeth's neck. She's dead.*

No!

*Leaving her lifeless body on the bed, The Creature springs up to a window. He taunts Victor.*

**Creature** That was good!

*Victor points his pistol but he can't pull the trigger.*

Shoot me. Go on. Kill me!

*The Creature laughs harshly and escapes through the window. Victor goes to Elizabeth's corpse and clutches at her. Clarice and the servants burst in.*

**Clarice** Sir!

**Victor** Pick her up! Bring her to my rooms!

**Clarice** Sir, she's dead!

**Victor** Carry her!

**Clarice** But sir, she's gone, she's –

**Victor** I can bring her back, Clarice, I can bring her back!

*He instructs three Servants to pick up Elizabeth. Clarice meanwhile runs out.*

Quickly! I have the equipment, I can reverse the process –
she is still warm and she has lost no blood! Quickly
there!

*The Servants carry Elizabeth to the door, and Victor
follows. Monsieur Frankenstein bursts in with Clarice.*

**Clarice** Sir, you must prevent him!

**M. Frankenstein** Victor, Victor, what have you done?
You are ill! Stop this at once!

**Clarice** She's dead, sir, quite dead!

**M. Frankenstein** Oh, my dear Elizabeth! – Did he kill
her?

**Victor** No, no, I –

**M. Frankenstein** Lay her on the bed and cover her. Now!

*The Servants do so.*

**Victor** I can bring her back. I have the skill.

**M. Frankenstein** What do you mean?

**Victor** I mean resurrect her. Trust me!

**M. Frankenstein** What are you saying?

**Clarice** He's gone mad, sir!

**Victor** I am not mad! I have powers beyond your
comprehension. How dare you call me mad?

**M. Frankenstein** Victor, this is not godly! I cannot bear
it!

*Victor calls out of the window to the Creature.*

**Victor** You! Whenever you look behind you, I'll be
there!

**M. Frankenstein** Restrain him.

*Victor tries to escape but is restrained.*

What have you done? First William, now Elizabeth. Death is everywhere! Your mind is disordered, it's –

**Victor** My mind is superb! It's superb!

**M. Frankenstein** Take him away. I can't look at him. He's monstrous!

*The Servants take Victor out. M. Frankenstein sinks to his knees and weeps terribly.*

Oh, dear God, forgive me!

**Clarice** Sir, be still.

**M. Frankenstein** What have I brought into the world?

**Clarice** You did your best.

**M. Frankenstein** I failed.


### SCENE THIRTY

*The polar ice-cap, inside the Arctic Circle. A blizzard howls. A huge moon dominates the scene.*
*The Creature wears nothing much, but he carries a sack. He is untroubled by the cold. He addresses us:*

**Creature** My heart is black. It stinks. My mind, once filled with dreams of beauty, is a furnace of revenge! Three years ago, when I was born, I laughed for joy at the heat of the sun, I cried at the call of the birds – the world was a cornucopia to me! Now it is a waste of frost and snow.

*From his sack the Creature takes silver cutlery, a plate, a pewter goblet, a napkin. He lays a place on the ice. He places strips of fresh meat on the plate, and fills the cup with wine from a flask.*

77

The son becomes the father, the master the slave. I have led him across the Black Sea, through Tartary and Russia. I have led him past Archangel, and out on to the ice. We go north, always north. His dogs are dead; his supplies exhausted. But we have a compact we must keep: he lives for my destruction, I live to lead him on. (*Calls into the wind.*) Frankenstein! Come! (*To us.*) I used to have dreams . . . I dreamt we were hiking, over the mountains, under a glorious sky. We would walk together, and talk together . . . he would tell me how to live. The mistakes to avoid. How to woo a girl. For this I came to find him, but he turned me away! Why did he do that? Why did he turn me away?

*Victor appears, wrapped in furs, frostbitten, harnessed to a dog-sled which he drags behind him.*

Come! What's the matter? Oh, are you cold? Do you feel forsaken?

*Victor is too exhausted to reply. He stumbles towards the Creature.*

Come, great explorer! Look – there is food. Seal meat! Explorers' food!

*Victor falls upon the food and devours it. The creature squats and watches from a distance.*

You wanted power. Look at you. Immortality. Look at you. Why did you treat me like a criminal?

**Victor** You killed my wife!

**Creature** You killed mine. Those who drove me from their doors, they're the criminals! – Oh, or are they virtuous Christians, and I an abortion to be kicked? Where's the logic in that? It's insulting in its stupidity! What fool said prejudice can be overcome?

**Victor** You have brought it upon yourself.

**Creature** Have I? How? How did I? Did I ask to be created? Did I ask you to make me from some muck in a sack? I am different, I know I am different! I have tried to be the same but I'm different! Why can I not be who I am? Why does humanity detest me? – The only one to show pity was Elizabeth. Lovely Elizabeth. I can still taste her lips, her strawberry lips . . . I can feel her warm breasts . . . her thighs . . .

*Victor tries to struggle to his feet. But he is too weak and he collapses.*

Up you get! We go on, on to the Pole! Let's find the source of the magnet! Let's make some discoveries! What do you say? Bring light to the darkness! Up! Up!

*Victor lies face down in the snow, still in his harness.*

Master?

*Victor remains still.*

Don't tell me you are dead already. Master? Don't you have more stamina than that? Why, we've hardly started!

*The Creature is worried.*

Don't leave me. Don't leave me alone. You and I, we are one.

*The Creature kneels and gently cradles Victor.*

While you live, I live. When you are gone, I must go too. Master, what is death? What will it feel like? Can I die?

*Victor remains still.*

Oh, Frankenstein. Will you forgive me my cruelty? Please forgive me. I am driven on, I cannot stop. The moon draws me on. The solitary moon! We can only go forward, we cannot go back. – Master! Drink! It's good wine. Drink.

*The Creature pours wine into his mouth. The claret runs into the snow. The Creature weeps.*

All I wanted was your love. I would have loved you with all my heart. My poor creator.

*Suddenly Victor revives.*

Master! You do love me! You do!

**Victor** (*very weakly*) I don't know what love is.

**Creature** I will teach you!

**Victor** Yes. You understand it better than I. Do you have a soul, and I none?

**Creature** (*elated*) I don't know! Let's debate!

**Victor** Every chance I had of love, I threw away. Every shred of human warmth, I cut to pieces. Hatred is what I understand. Nothingness. Despair. I am finished. – But you give me purpose. You, I desire. Go on. Walk on. You must be destroyed!

**Creature** Good boy. That's the spirit! Bring my miserable line to an end! Up! Up!

*The Creature backs away. With a superhuman effort, Victor struggles to his feet, heaves his sledge, and follows.*

Come, scientist! Destroy me! Destroy your creation! Come!

*They exit into the icy distance, the Creature prancing in front of Victor, who struggles after him.*

*The End.*